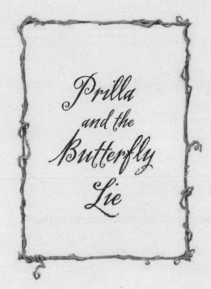

Prilla
and the
Butterfly
Lie

Tinker Bell
Takes
Charge

PaRragon

Bath · New York · Singapore · Hong Kong · Cologne · Delhi · Melbourne

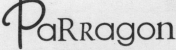

First published by Parragon in 2008
Parragon
Queen Street House
4 Queen Street
Bath BA1 1HE, UK

ISBN 978-1-4075-2217-3

Printed in UK

All About Fairies

IF YOU HEAD towards the second star on your right and fly straight on till morning, you'll come to Never Land, a magical island where mermaids play and children never grow up.

When you arrive, you might hear something like the tinkling of little bells. Follow that sound and you'll find Pixie Hollow, the secret heart of Never Land.

A great old maple tree grows in Pixie Hollow, and in it live hundreds of fairies and sparrow men. Some of them can do water magic, others can fly like the wind, and still others can speak to animals. You see, Pixie Hollow is the Never fairies' kingdom, and each fairy who lives there has a special, extraordinary talent.

Not far from the Home Tree, nestled in the branches of a hawthorn, is Mother Dove, the most magical creature of all. She sits on her egg, watching over the fairies, who in turn watch over her. For as long as Mother Dove's egg stays well and whole, no one in Never Land will ever grow old.

Once, Mother Dove's egg *was* broken. But we are not telling the story of the egg here. Now it is time for Prilla and Tinker Bell's tales…

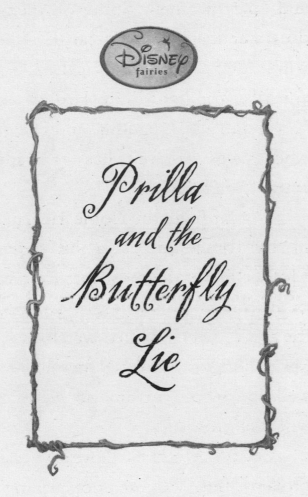

Disney fairies

Prilla
and the
Butterfly
Lie

PRILLA KNELT ON the library shelf. She put her hands over her mouth to hold back her laughter. She kept her eyes on a little girl in pigtails who stood on her tiptoes, reaching for a book.

The girl grabbed the book and slid it off the shelf. Quick as a wink, Prilla popped out from the space where the book had been. The little girl stared at Prilla for a moment. Then she squealed with delight, her blue eyes wide.

"A fairy!"

"Shhh!" said the librarian. She gave the girl a stern look. Prilla giggled. She turned a somersault in the air and...

"Grab him, Prilla!" a voice cried.

Suddenly, Prilla was in a sunny meadow, back in Pixie Hollow. Nettle, a caterpillar-shearing-talent fairy, stood in front of her, holding a pair of shears. Nettle pointed to the caterpillar that Prilla was supposed to be keeping still. The caterpillar was bucking around like a little green bronco. It had knocked over a sack of caterpillar fuzz.

Prilla sighed. It had been a long and trying day. She was very fond of Nettle, which was why she had found it hard to refuse when Nettle had asked her if she would like to give caterpillar shearing a try.

The day had started well enough. Nettle gave Prilla a tour of the caterpillar corral. First they had seen some caterpillars hatching from eggs. Then they'd watched a few caterpillars shedding their skin. Next they had seen some furry caterpillars making their cocoons.

Suddenly, Nettle had grabbed Prilla's arm. "We're just in time to watch a butterfly hatch!" she'd whispered.

Prilla had held her breath as they'd silently watched the butterfly emerge from its cocoon. She was amazed that a funny-looking caterpillar could transform into such a beautiful creature.

Watching the butterfly hatch had been exciting. But Prilla had quickly realised that shearing caterpillars was not. Her job was to hold the caterpillars while Nettle clipped their fuzz with her shears. Prilla tried hard to help. But the truth was that she didn't really like shearing caterpillars at all. It was hot in the sun. It was dull doing the same thing over and over again. But most of all, Prilla just didn't like caterpillars. Not one bit. They were prickly. They were kind of ugly. And they were grumpy.

Bored, Prilla had finally allowed herself to drift off and blink over to the mainland. Prilla was a mainland-visiting clapping-talent fairy, the only one in Pixie Hollow. In the blink of an eye, she could zip from Never Land to the mainland to visit children. Prilla's talent was very important, for it kept children's belief in fairies alive. When children didn't believe in them, fairies died.

But Prilla didn't visit the mainland only to save fairies' lives. She also went because it was her favourite thing in the world to do.

And look what had happened! She hadn't been paying attention, and now things were getting out of control.

Prilla leaned forward to grab the cranky caterpillar around its middle. It wiggled away from her, and Prilla stumbled. The other shearing-talent fairies chuckled in sympathy.

"He's a wild one, he is," said Jason, a caterpillar-shearing-talent sparrow man.

Prilla tried once again to seize the creature. The caterpillar reared up. Prilla lost her balance and fell backwards. She landed in the grass with a soft thump.

"Don't worry, Prilla. You can do it!" Jason called, noticing the frown on Prilla's face.

Still the restless caterpillar wiggled. "There, there," said Nettle in a soothing voice. She put down her shears.

Nettle's gentle tone calmed the caterpillar. It began to settle down. Prilla stood and brushed herself off. Not knowing what else to do, she bent to pat the caterpillar on the head.

Quickly, Nettle began to shear the caterpillar. In a couple of minutes, she had finished. "That wasn't so bad, was it?" she asked.

Prilla wasn't sure if Nettle was talking to her or to the caterpillar. She shook her head anyway.

Nettle let the newly shorn caterpillar go. Prilla watched as it inched away as fast as it could – which was pretty slow.

Nettle smiled at Prilla. "You sit and rest," she said. "I'll do the cleaning up."

Prilla lowered herself onto a moss-covered stone. She picked a stray piece of caterpillar fuzz from the hem of her pale pink silk skirt. Nettle and the other caterpillar shearers began sweeping up the loose fuzz.

Thank goodness that's over, Prilla thought. *Maybe tomorrow I won't do anything but blink over to the mainland as many times as I want.* It would be a perfect day.

Nettle put the caterpillar fuzz she'd swept up into a sack made of woven grass. She tied it shut with a flourish.

Then she loaded it onto a wheelbarrow full of sacks.

Jason picked up the handles of the wheelbarrow. He set off with the load towards the Home Tree, the towering maple tree where the fairies lived and worked. "Have fun, Prilla. Thanks for your help!" he cried.

"Fly safely, Jason!" said Prilla. She waved.

Nettle sat next to her on the stone and patted Prilla's knee. "What a great day," Nettle said. "I could tell how much you enjoyed it."

"Well, I – " Prilla began.

"Being outside, working with those wonderful caterpillars." Nettle leaned in close to Prilla. She lowered her voice as if she were about to tell her a secret. "Other talents might argue with me, but caterpillar shearing really is the most important talent. Wouldn't you agree?"

She went on, not waiting for Prilla to answer. "First of all, it helps the caterpillars grow nice woolly coats for when it's time to build their cocoons. And then there're all the great things we make out of the fuzz!" She began to list them on her fingers. "Soft pillows, cosy comforters, light-as-a-feather blankets, thick sweaters, those wonderful linens..." Her voice trailed off.

Prilla nodded. She liked pillows, comforters, blankets, sweaters, and linens as much as the next fairy did. It seemed that caterpillar shearing was indeed very important.

"Yes, it is a lovely talent," she said out

loud. *I just hope I never have to help shear another caterpillar ever again!* she silently added. She leaned back on her elbows.

And before Prilla knew it, she had blinked over to the mainland. She saw a little girl holding a fluffy white dandelion. The girl pursed her lips to blow the seeds. Prilla flew towards her...

"I said, what do you think?" Nettle said suddenly.

Prilla started. Nettle was looking at her expectantly.

"Sorry, can you repeat that?" Prilla asked.

And then Nettle said the dreaded words: "Same time tomorrow?"

2

PRILLA'S HEART SANK. She stared at Nettle's hopeful face. *No, thank you,* she said in her head. *I have other plans. I don't like caterpillars. I don't like them at all.* She just didn't say the words out loud.

"Why, sure," Prilla found herself saying. "I'd be happy to help you out again."

"Great!" said Nettle. "I knew you'd love my talent as much as I do!"

Nettle stood and picked up the last sack of caterpillar fuzz. She slung it over her shoulder and headed back to the Home Tree, whistling merrily.

Well, that didn't go very well, Prilla thought. *And it certainly changes my plans for tomorrow!* She'd have to blink over to the mainland that night after dinner instead.

As she got up to leave, the still evening air was stirred by a sudden brisk breeze. Out of the corner of her eye, Prilla saw a flash of purple. And there, standing in front of her, was Vidia.

"Hello, dearest," said Vidia. "Did you have a nice day today? Do something fun?" Her tone was mocking, as usual.

"Well, I – " Prilla began.

"Come, darling. Let's go for a walk, shall we?" Without waiting for Prilla's response, Vidia set off at a quick pace.

Prilla stared at Vidia's retreating back in confusion. As the fastest of the fast-flying-talent fairies, Vidia never walked when she could fly. It went against her nature.

What is going on? Prilla wondered. She followed Vidia to find out, racing to catch up. Even on land, Vidia was fast.

Finally, Vidia came to a stop at the edge of a minnow pond. It was nearly sunset, and the sky was a soft shade of pinkish purple. There was a pleasant chorus of chirping crickets and peeping frogs. Fireflies had begun lighting up the dusky air around them.

Vidia turned to face Prilla. "So what have you been up to lately, dearest?" she asked.

"Oh, a little of this, a little of that," Prilla answered.

"Mmm-hmm," replied Vidia. She had a funny look on her face, as if she was trying not to smirk. "A little tree-bark grading?" Vidia asked sweetly.

Prilla nodded. She remembered the splinters she had got that day.

"Maybe some floor polishing?" Vidia went on.

Prilla winced. She had spent an entire afternoon on her hands and knees, helping polish the mica entryway in the Home Tree.

"And some dandelion-fluff sorting?"

"That made me sneeze," Prilla recalled. She was beginning to feel self-conscious. Had she *really* been spending that much time helping out other talents?

She cleared her throat to speak. But Vidia wasn't finished.

"And then a little caterpillar shearing today... Look, Prilla," Vidia said. She put her hands on her hips. "I've been trying to ignore it, but your nicey-nice behaviour is getting on my last nerve. I've got a new talent for you, sweetness — doormat talent. You let everyone walk all over you."

Prilla cringed. Was she really that bad?

"Don't look at me as if I've been pulling the wings off dragonflies. I know everyone around here thinks I'm horrible, but I do try to help out a fellow fairy now and then. So I'm helping you now. I don't want to see you hurt."

Vidia scowled fiercely. Prilla had the feeling Vidia hadn't meant to say that last part.

Raising her chin, Vidia flipped her hair back and said, "Face it, Prilla, you've got a problem."

"A problem? What do you mean, Vidia?" asked Prilla.

"You are the fairy who just can't say no."

Prilla stared at her shoes. "Well, what's wrong with being helpful?" she asked, a little defensively.

She didn't want to say it out loud to Vidia, but she *liked* it when other fairies asked her for help. In Pixie Hollow, talent groups did everything together. They worked together, played together, ate their meals together. When Prilla had first arrived, she hadn't known what her talent was. She had felt very alone.

Prilla had desperately wanted to fit in back then. In the end, she'd found her talent and her place among the fairies. But even now, every time someone asked for her help, she felt glad.

She knew that Vidia would never understand. Vidia was a loner. She preferred her own company to that of anyone else. Why, she even lived alone in a sour-plum tree, apart from the rest of the fairies.

Vidia gave Prilla an exasperated look. "Sweetness, what is the only thing that's important to me?" she asked.

That wasn't hard to answer. "Flying fast, of course," Prilla replied.

"And why is that?" Vidia asked.

Prilla was puzzled. "Because you like to... fly quickly?"

Vidia rolled her eyes. "Because it's my *talent*, pumpkin. The most important thing to any fairy is her talent." She crossed her arms and smirked at Prilla. "But the most important thing to you, apparently, is being helpful!" Vidia made a disgusted face as she said the word "helpful."

With a sinking heart, Prilla realised that Vidia was right. She had been spending too much time on other fairies' talents and not enough time on her own.

"But I don't like to say no," Prilla admitted. "I don't want to hurt anyone's feelings."

"Why not just say, 'Be gone with you! Your stupid talent bores me!'?" Vidia suggested.

Prilla gasped. "You know I could never say that!"

"Okay, okay," Vidia said. "Maybe that isn't your style. But the next time a fairy asks you to help with some dreadful task, you should say, 'Forget it. I'm not interested. I have my own talent to attend to.'"

Prilla frowned. "Why do you care, Vidia? Why do you want to help me?"

Vidia paused. Then she shrugged. "You helped me once. I'm just returning the favour."

And quick as a wink, she was gone.

Prilla walked home slowly, deep in thought. Vidia was right. Prilla was not a caterpillar-shearing fairy. She wasn't a tree-bark-grading fairy. Or an entryway-polishing fairy. Or one of any of those other talents.

Prilla was the one and only mainland-visiting clapping-talent fairy. And it was time she started acting like it.

3

THE MORNING SUNLIGHT crept into Prilla's room, waking her. She yawned and stretched.

Feeling very lazy, she located a few grains of fairy dust and, from her bed, sprinkled some on her washing-up items. Magically, the pitcher poured water – not too hot, not too cold, but just right – into the washing bowl. A velvety moss washcloth dipped itself into the warm water, wrung itself out, and gently scrubbed her face. She giggled as it washed behind her ears. It tickled.

Next she flicked a grain onto her pine needle–bristle hairbrush. Exactly twenty-five strokes later, her hair was glossy and tangle free. Prilla considered using fairy dust to get dressed. She laughed at the thought of her clothes marching out of the wardrobe and modelling themselves for her as she considered each outfit.

Instead, Prilla climbed out of bed and made her way to her wardrobe. She took off her whisper-soft white muslin nightgown and put on her favourite pink silk dress with purple trim. After fastening its leafy green belt around her tiny waist, she began to search for her matching shoes. Finally, she found them far underneath her bed. She pulled the buckles tightly around her ankles. Now she was ready to face the day.

She skipped out of her room. In the hallway, she nearly bumped into Cinda, one of Queen Clarion's helper fairies.

"Excuse me, Cinda," Prilla said. But Cinda seemed to be in a rush and hardly noticed.

On Prilla's way to the tearoom, her stomach rumbled. She smiled when she saw the breakfast that Dulcie and the rest of the baking-talent fairies had made. There were chocolate turnovers, acorn bread, lemon poppy-seed rolls, blueberry muffins, and cinnamon twists. There were several different spreads – honey butter, pumpkin butter, and maple butter, plus strawberry, gooseberry, chokecherry, and beach plum jams. Steaming pots of peppermint tea sat next to icy pitchers of raspberry, blueberry, and sparkling red Never berry juice on the table.

Prilla smiled again as she recalled the time she'd helped out in the kitchen.

"Anyone can learn to bake!" Dulcie had insisted. After a fallen cake, a dozen rock-hard muffins, and two baking sheets of burnt, misshapen cookies, Dulcie had been forced to admit defeat. "I guess some fairies aren't meant to bake after all," she had said with a shake of her head.

Prilla scanned the room, looking for a place to sit. It was a busy morning in the tearoom. She thought she'd like to catch up with her friend Rani, but the water-talent table was full. So was the pots-and-pans-talent table, so she couldn't sit with Tinker Bell, either. She saw an empty chair at the garden-talent table, where her friend Lily was sitting. But then Rosetta took the seat. Finally, Prilla spotted an open place at the decoration-talent table and headed towards it.

"Yoo-hoo! Prilla!" called a familiar voice. Nettle waved to her from across the room.

Oh, no, Prilla thought. She had planned to tell Nettle the bad news *after* breakfast. But then she shrugged. *I might as well get it over with,* she thought. She took a deep breath and headed towards the caterpillar shearers table.

"Our honorary caterpillar shearer!" gushed Jason. "We're looking forward to working with you again today."

Nettle patted the seat next to her. "Sit down," she said. She noticed Prilla hesitate. "What's the matter, Prilla?" she asked.

Now was the perfect time to tell her. But Prilla didn't know how to begin.

"Are you ill?" Nettle asked.

Prilla shook her head. She gulped. "Actually, I have to be honest with you, Nettle," she said.

"Yes?" said Nettle. Her hazel eyes widened.

"Here's the thing about caterpillars… ," Prilla began. She opened her mouth to say, "I don't like them." But nothing came out. She couldn't say the words aloud.

Nettle smiled. "I know," she said. "Aren't they great?"

Prilla lost her nerve. "Yes," she fibbed. "Caterpillars *are* great." Then she had an idea. "But there's something I like even better."

"What is it?" asked Nettle. "What could possibly be even better than caterpillars?"

Prilla bit her lip. Her mind was a complete blank. "I like... " She frantically tried to think of something. *Think, Prilla, think!* She stared out of the window for inspiration.

At that moment, a pretty pink and blue butterfly flitted past. "Butterflies!" Prilla said triumphantly. "I like butterflies!" She felt relieved for a split second. Then she thought, *Butterflies? Why did I just say that?*

Nettle gave her a puzzled look. "Butterflies?" she finally said. "Are you sure?"

It was too late to change her answer now. "Yes, I'm sure," Prilla said, nodding. "Lovely butterflies. I just can't get enough of them. Such colourful, delicate creatures. They fly, you know. All over the place. Fascinating," she babbled.

"Butterflies," Nettle said. "How unusual." She shook her head, as if to clear it. "That's very… interesting." Nettle paused for a moment. "Well, I guess you won't be helping us with the caterpillars today, then?"

"I guess not," said Prilla. "I'll be focusing on… butterflies."

Nettle's brow wrinkled. "If you say so," she said.

"See you later, Nettle," said Prilla. She crossed the room and found an empty seat at the keyhole-design table. As she sat down, she braced herself for someone to ask her to help design keyholes.

But to her relief, no one did. Instead,

the fairies at the table chatted about the designs they were planning to create that day. Prilla smiled and ate her breakfast in silence.

She took a big bite of a roll. Light and flaky and buttery – delicious. The jam was both tart and sweet. *Mmm.* She had forgotten how hungry she was.

As she ate, she thought about what she had told Nettle. Not being truthful to Nettle had been wrong. But Prilla had only done it to spare her friend's feelings. There was no reason to think about it anymore. It was over and done with.

That is the end of that, Prilla thought.

4

THAT EVENING AT DINNER, Prilla sat quietly by herself. She thought about all the adventures she'd had that day blinking over to the mainland. She had surprised a little girl struggling over a homework problem. She'd cheered up a boy who'd been kept after school for talking in class. She had played peekaboo with a baby, who had screamed with delight.

She had also visited a toy store, where she had amused young shoppers by sitting in the engine of a toy train. Then she'd hidden behind a stack of sugar cones in an ice cream parlour. She had flown to the top of a Ferris wheel and made faces at the riders. Later, she'd sat on a little girl's shoulder at the circus while clowns tumbled and cheerful music played.

Ding, ding, ding, ding, ding! Prilla looked up to see Cinda tapping her water glass with a fork. A hush fell over the tearoom. That was the signal that Queen Clarion, the leader of all the Never fairies, had an important announcement to make.

Queen Clarion, lovely and regal, as always, swept into the room. *She seems a bit anxious*, Prilla thought, sitting up straight in her chair.

"My fellow fairies," Queen Clarion said, "I don't want to alarm anyone, but I have some rather unpleasant news to share with you this evening." She paused for a moment. "I am sorry to tell you that there has been an outbreak of fairy pox."

There was a sharp collective intake of breath.

"Several of your fellow fairies have already been infected," the queen went on.

The room began to buzz. Some of the newer fairies asked the older fairies to explain what fairy pox was. There hadn't been an outbreak of fairy pox in Pixie Hollow in many years. But it was hard to miss a fairy with the pox. The fairies who got it broke out into spots. The spots could be quite pretty – pale pink, blue, and purple. But fairy pox made fairies dangerously sleepy. A fairy could fall asleep at the table and drown in her soup bowl if she wasn't careful! Luckily, with plenty of bed rest and a daily dose of daisy pollen, fairies were almost always cured.

Over the noise, the queen said, "Fairy pox may not be life threatening, but it is very contagious. All ill fairies have been moved to the infirmary. Only nursing-talent fairies are allowed to have contact with sick fairies. So the rest of you, please keep your distance from anyone who is ill."

There was silence. The fairies began to check each other for the telltale spots.

Bess, an art-talent fairy, looked down at her paint-speckled arms. "I forgot to wash up before dinner!" she explained. The rest of the fairies at her table laughed nervously. Then they shifted away from her, just a bit.

Iris, a garden-talent fairy who had

been up all night searching for a rare shrinking violet, let out a jaw-popping yawn. She was surprised when her tablemates on both sides of her hastily excused themselves and found seats at another table.

Queen Clarion looked around the room. "Are there any questions?"

"Can you tell us who is sick?" a light-talent sparrow man asked.

Queen Clarion gestured towards the nursing-talent table. "Poppy, would you like to give an update?" she asked.

Poppy, a jolly nursing-talent fairy, stood up. "There are a dozen sick fairies so far." She began listing them on her fingers. "Olivia, Heather, Flora, Marigold, Jordan, Zuzu, Amaryllis, Rhia, Aidan, Russell, Violet, and Primrose are

33

ill," she reported. "But they are all resting comfortably. They are sleeping a lot, as you can imagine! Why, just the other night, Jordan was telling a marvellous story about a battle between Captain Hook and a sea serpent. He fell sound asleep just as he got to the best part! I was almost tempted to wake him up to see what happened next!"

Everyone laughed. Jordan was one of the finest storytelling-talent fairies.

"So you see, your friends are in good hands. They'll soon be as good as new." Poppy sat down.

Queen Clarion spoke again. "So if there are no more questions, the serving-talent fairies can bring in the first – "

"Wait! Wait!" Jason interrupted. He stood up. "It looks like each and every one of the butterfly herders is sick! All eight of them!"

Heads swung around to peer at the butterfly herders' table. Sure enough, it was empty!

A look of alarm crossed the queen's face. The butterflies were important to the fairies, since they laid the eggs that became caterpillars. If anything were to happen to the butterfly herd, the fairies wouldn't have any caterpillars – or any caterpillar fuzz.

"Well," the queen said, "I am sure we'll have no problem getting volunteers to help with the butterfly herding until they are able to return to work. Would anyone like to pitch in?" She looked around hopefully.

An uncomfortable silence filled the

tearoom. Some fairies studied their forks. Others examined their dinner plates very closely. No one would look up.

"No volunteers," said the queen. "This is indeed a problem. What are we to do?"

"I know!" said a voice. "There is a fairy who would be happy to help out. She *loves* butterflies."

The room began to buzz once more. Everyone wondered who the butterfly-loving fairy could be.

Prilla sank into her chair until her head was barely level with the table. She had completely forgotten about her butterfly lie.

"And who is this fairy?" Queen Clarion asked.

"It's Prilla!" said Nettle. "She told me

she likes butterflies even better than caterpillars!" she announced.

Prilla stared at the tablecloth. Her glow turned orange as she blushed. She felt every fairy in the tearoom peering at her curiously.

Even the queen looked surprised. "Is this true, Prilla?" she asked.

Without looking up, Prilla spoke. "Yes, it's true," she said miserably. "I did tell Nettle that."

When Prilla finally raised her head, she found herself looking right at Vidia, who was directly across the room. Vidia rolled her eyes and shook her head. Prilla could just imagine what she was thinking – that silly little fairy had gone and done it again!

5

KNOCK! KNOCK! KNOCK!

"Rise and shine, Prilla! It's time to start your day!" a wake-up-talent fairy called through the door.

Prilla struggled to open her eyes. Was it morning already? Hadn't she *just* fallen asleep? The sun was not even up yet!

Butterfly-herding talents certainly start their day very early, Prilla thought. She groaned and rolled out of bed.

She was still half-asleep as she pulled a simple cotton dress over her head. She didn't even notice that she put on two different kinds of socks or that her dress was buttoned wrong.

She picked up her hairbrush. She

remembered how the queen had smiled at her gratefully the night before. "Good luck tomorrow," the queen had said. "Never butterflies are beautiful creatures, my dear. But of course, they are prone to ... " She stopped and shook her head. "But you know all about butterflies – you love them! You'll have no problem at all!"

Prone to what? Prilla had wanted to ask. But she couldn't let on that she didn't know anything about looking after butterflies.

Sighing, Prilla set down her hairbrush and headed downstairs.

Dulcie met Prilla at the front door, holding a small sack. She laughed when she saw Prilla's sleepy face and mismatched socks.

Dulcie handed Prilla the sack. "Your

breakfast," she said.

A dust-talent fairy was waiting outside with Prilla's daily dose of fairy dust. She sprinkled a level teacup of dust – not a smidgen more or a smidgen less – over Prilla. As usual, it was shivery and cool as it settled on Prilla's head and shoulders.

"Thank you," Prilla said. She slung the sack over her shoulder, took a deep breath, and rose into the air.

The sun was coming up over the hills. The meadow was starting to buzz with the sound of insects. Prilla began to feel better. *I'm herding butterflies, not water snakes, for goodness' sake!* she told herself. *How hard can it be?*

Woods, valleys, meadows, streams, ponds, and colourful flowers all stretched out beneath her. Prilla turned a few aerial cartwheels and laughed with joy. There was something exciting about being up before everyone else. It made the day seem filled with adventure and possibility.

Prilla spied the garden-talent fairies' flower-filled gardens. She could pick out Lily's garden by the orange and red poppies, which were the biggest in Pixie Hollow. Prilla flew over the part of Havendish Stream where the water talents sometimes gathered. Looking back, she could see the Home Tree, small in the distance.

She looked down as she passed over a clearing. To her delight, she spotted the herd of butterflies!

Prilla hovered in the air, drinking in

the scene. There were about fifty of the delicate creatures. Their wings beat lazily as they sunned themselves in the early-morning warmth.

And the colours! They took Prilla's breath away. There were shades of red, orange, yellow, green, blue, violet, shimmery gold, burnished copper, and shining silver. They were more beautiful than the biggest and brightest rainbow Prilla had ever seen.

The sun was barely up and she'd already found the butterflies. *Why, this is going to be easy!* Prilla smiled. She'd be finished so early, she would have plenty of time for a nap and a blink over to the mainland before dinner.

Taking a deep breath, she landed quietly in the middle of the butterfly herd. That was when she realised she wasn't sure what to do next. Finding the group was one thing. But Prilla didn't know the first thing about herding them.

"Um, hello, butterflies," she said uncertainly. Prilla knew that the butterflies weren't able to understand her. But that didn't stop her from talking to them anyway. "I'll be your herder today. Our first stop will be Flower Field," she said.

Flower Field was a nearby meadow filled with wildflowers of all shapes, sizes, and colours – stately Queen Anne's lace, snappy black-eyed Susans, lovely Indian paintbrush. It seemed like a perfect place for butterflies

"So let's go!" Prilla said, clapping her hands.

And to her delight, all the butterflies lifted off into the air!

How wonderful! Prilla thought as they rose. They began to circle. *So far, so good.*

But without warning, the butterflies started to turn off in different directions. Prilla's heart sank. This wasn't how it was supposed to be!

"Hey, wait!" Prilla shouted. She chased after a blue and purple butterfly and waved her hands to get it to stay with the others.

But just as she reached it, the butterfly dropped several inches in the air. Prilla found herself headed right for a tree branch! At the last second, she ducked under it.

Just then, she noticed that a tiny silvery yellow butterfly had got quite far away from the others. That wouldn't do at all! Prilla took off after it and chased it back to the herd.

But the butterflies wouldn't stay together. Prilla hovered in the air, staring at them. She wondered what she was doing wrong. This was exhausting!

Suddenly, Prilla noticed that the butterflies were starting to move closer together. She watched with pleasure as they formed one large group. "That's more like it," she said.

Just as she was about to try to shepherd them to Flower Field, she realised that the herd of butterflies had started to pick up speed. They were headed right for her!

"Stop! Stop!" Prilla cried. But they kept coming, all fifty of them. It would have been beautiful if it hadn't been so frightening!

In a second, the butterflies were upon her. They surrounded her on all sides. Prilla felt the breeze from one hundred beating wings.

"Hey… wait… what are you doing?" she said. She found herself being jostled and pushed.

The next thing she knew, she felt rough tree bark against her back. Suddenly, the butterflies broke apart. Prilla was dangling from a branch high above the ground.

What happened? Prilla thought. She tried to turn around, but she couldn't. Then she understood. Her belt had got caught on a twig. She was stuck.

Prilla watched as the swarm of butterflies merrily flew away, flitting and fluttering. She gazed after them until they were merely a colourful band across the sky. Finally, they disappeared from her sight.

"This is a fine mess you've gotten yourself into, Prilla," she scolded herself.

She sighed. The ground was a long way down. Squirm as she might, she wasn't budging an inch. Butterfly herding had certainly got off to a disappointing start!

6

A SLIGHT BREEZE BLEW, and Prilla swayed back and forth in the air. She wondered how she was going to get down. Thank goodness no one was around to see her!

"Prilla!" someone shouted.

Oh dear, Prilla thought. *How embarassing to be caught like this!* She looked down at the ground. Pluck, a harvest-talent fairy, was staring up at her. Her hands were on her hips. Her mouth formed an O of surprise.

"Prilla! What are you doing up there?" Pluck called up.

"Oh, I'm just scouting for butterflies!" Prilla cried. She cupped her hand over her eyes and scanned the horizon. "Nope! Haven't spotted any yet! But just give me time! I'll be herding them here and there before you know it!"

Pluck flew up to hover near Prilla's branch. Prilla gulped and gave Pluck a big fake smile that was meant to say, "Things may look a bit out of the ordinary to you, but really, everything is perfectly fine."

But Pluck was having none of that. She looked closely at Prilla and frowned. "It looks to me like you're stuck!"

Prilla laughed nervously. "Oh, no, this is my special lookout twig," she explained. "Don't you worry about me!"

She crossed her arms and smiled, even though her belt was digging into her waist. She decided to change the subject. "So what are you up to today?" she asked.

Pluck gave Prilla an odd look. Then she shrugged and began to explain. "There were reports of a gigantic bush full of plump, juicy blackberries near Flower Field," she said. "Have you spotted it?"

Prilla shook her head. "But I'll be sure to let you know if I do." She frowned at Pluck. Why wasn't she leaving? "So, good luck finding the bush!" Prilla said enthusiastically. "Blackberries, how delicious!"

"Thanks," said Pluck. She seemed to be thinking about something. "I know! Why don't you leave your lookout twig for a while and come with me?" she suggested. "Never butterflies love berries, you know. Maybe the herd will be there. Then you can help me harvest the berries.

And I can help you herd the butterflies!"

It was a good idea. Herding butterflies would be so much easier with two fairies instead of one. But Prilla couldn't move without admitting that she was stuck. And then she would have to explain the embarrassing way she had come to be stuck. As far as Prilla was concerned, that was not an option.

"Oh, it's okay," said Prilla. "I think I'll stay right here for the time being." She smiled as if she hadn't a care in the world.

"Whatever suits you," said Pluck. Then she grinned at Prilla. "Those butterflies are something else, aren't they?" she said. "I have so much respect for the butterfly talents. We were all so happy when you volunteered!"

She leaned over and gave Prilla a playful tap on the shoulder. Prilla swung gently from side to side. "You are one brave fairy!" Pluck said.

Prilla's eyes widened. Brave? What did Pluck mean? But to ask would be the same as saying, "I have no idea what you are talking about. And that's because I told a lie to Nettle – and to the queen!" So Prilla just laughed uneasily. She mumbled a farewell. And Pluck, with one backwards glance at Prilla, finally took off.

A short while later, Prilla was safely on the ground. She had finally decided to undo the belt and hope that she could start flying before she hit the ground. Luckily, she was quite high up, and this wasn't a problem.

That was a close one! Prilla thought. She would have to be more careful in the future.

Now she needed to find the butterflies again. Where could they have gone? Prilla decided to visit Lily's garden. All those fruits and flowers would be certain to attract butterflies – or so she thought.

But as she flew over the garden, Prilla saw that she was wrong. There wasn't a butterfly to be seen.

Lily saw Prilla hovering overhead. She put down her hoe and waved Prilla over. Prilla cupped her hands around her mouth and called down to her friend, "I can't stop now! I'll be back later!"

Lily nodded and went back to work. How Prilla envied Lily. She got to spend her day doing what she loved most!

Prilla took a sharp turn and headed to Marigold Meadow. She saw many fat honeybees but not a single butterfly. Next she went to the spot where the sweetest bunch of clover in all of Pixie Hollow grew. But there were no butterflies there, either.

Puzzled, Prilla landed and began to search more slowly. She peeked inside hollow logs. She lifted cabbage leaves to search underneath them. She looked inside cool dark caves. She even searched among the long grasses that grew near the shoreline. But there wasn't a single butterfly to be found.

Prilla sat down and leaned against the hollow shell. *It's almost as if they're hiding from me,* she thought. Then she laughed.

What a silly idea!

She closed her eyes for a split second. Without even thinking about it, Prilla blinked over to the mainland.

What fun! She was in a nursery school class with dozens of children. She flew into a castle that a girl was building out of blocks. Prilla waved to the girl from a turret. Then she flew over to two boys who were each pulling on one end of a teddy bear. Prilla got their attention by doing loop-de-loops in the air. The teddy bear fell to the ground, completely forgotten.

Prilla was heading over to the doll corner when she felt someone shaking her shoulder.

"Prilla, are you okay?" a familiar voice asked.

7

PRILLA LOOKED AROUND. She was sitting on the ground. Her hands were behind her. And – *Oh dear*, Prilla thought – Pluck was back. She was looking at Prilla anxiously.

"Are you okay?" Pluck asked again. Her brow wrinkled in concern. "Oh – were you blinking to the mainland? Did I bother you?"

Prilla shook her head. "It's fine," she said.

"I found the blackberries!" Pluck said proudly. She held up a basket filled to the brim with three berries. "Would you like one?"

Prilla nodded. Pluck held out a

big juicy berry. But as Prilla tried to reach for it, she discovered something very odd indeed. She couldn't move her hands. They were stuck together behind her back!

This is strange, Prilla thought. She struggled mightily. Her hands wouldn't budge. *Could they be tied together?* she wondered. *But how? And why?*

Pluck continued to hold out the berry. An annoyed frown started to form on her face. Prilla couldn't explain her predicament to Pluck, since she herself had no idea what was going on. But she knew that it would be rude not to take a bite of the berry since she had asked for it. Not knowing what else to do, Prilla opened her mouth like a hungry baby bird.

Pluck's expression changed from annoyed to puzzled. She held the berry to Prilla's mouth. Prilla bit into it. The juices dripped down her chin.

"Delicious," Prilla said, trying to act as if eating like this was completely normal. She took another bite. "Mmmm."

When Prilla had eaten her fill, Pluck quickly said goodbye. She headed off towards the Home Tree with the remaining berries. *Pluck will have an interesting story to tell when she gets back!* Prilla thought with a giggle. *She must think I am very odd indeed!*

After much struggling, Prilla was finally able to slip her wrists free. She discovered that they had been bound with thick threads of spider silk. *How did that happen?* Prilla wondered. *Did some spider mistake me for an extra-large fly? Was I about to become a spider's next meal?* That was a scary thought! She had never heard of a spider capturing and devouring a Never fairy before. But she guessed that anything was possible.

Well, no use worrying about what could have happened, Prilla thought. She was safe and sound, at least for the moment. But what an odd day she was having!

Prilla started walking again, looking in all the usual places that a butterfly might choose to hide in. She looked in knotholes in trees, under dead leaves, in between rocks. Then she spied a flash of colour from the corner of her eye.

Prilla ran forward and peeked into the tall grass. There sat a butterfly. It was the tiny silvery yellow creature that she had chased earlier.

Prilla smiled widely. She felt incredible relief.

The butterfly opened and closed its wings slowly. It was so close that Prilla could see every colourful scale on its wings. It was so close that she could reach out and…

Her movement startled the butterfly. It took off, then landed a couple of inches away.

Prilla sighed in frustration. But then she was surprised to see the butterfly turn around. She quietly crept up to it. But the butterfly wouldn't stay put. It flew a short distance, then landed, flew a short distance, then landed, over and over again.

They went on like this for quite a while, Prilla following closely. Once, she lost sight of the butterfly. Her heart sank, and her eyes started to fill with tears. But then it reappeared right in front of her. It was almost as if the butterfly had been looking for her.

Suddenly, the butterfly flew away into a thicket. Prilla ran up and parted the leaves. She hadn't lost it after all this, had she?

To her surprise, she had discovered a small clearing. And there were the butterflies – all fifty of them!

Prilla grinned. *Take it slowly this time,* she told herself. *Try not to make any sudden movements that will startle them. Everything is going to be all right.*

Just then, Prilla felt a tickle in her

nose. *Oh, no! I can't sneeze now,* she thought. *That will scare them away again!* She wrinkled her nose to make the itch go away. She held her nose, but nothing worked. What was wrong with her?

Then she noticed the leaves on the bushes around her. She was standing right in the middle of a patch of sneezewort!

Ah-ah-ah-CHOO! Prilla sneezed so hard, she nearly knocked herself over. *Ah-choo, ah-choo, ah-choo!*

Finally, her sneezing fit ended. Prilla was not surprised to find that she had scared the entire butterfly herd away – again. She backed away from the sneezewort patch. Noisily, she blew her nose into a leafkerchief.

Prilla shook her head. What bad luck she was having!

8

PRILLA'S STOMACH RUMBLED. She had been searching for the butterflies for quite a while, and she was awfully hungry. It was time to eat her breakfast.

Spotting a table-sized toadstool, Prilla landed next to it. She began to unpack the food that Dulcie had given her that morning. She was pleased to find two strawberry muffins, a clay thermos full of hot tea with honey and lemon, and a cobweb napkin. Prilla sprinkled some fairy dust on a smooth, round stone. She floated it over to the toadstool table for a comfortable place to sit.

Just as she was about to take a seat, a

breeze blew her napkin off the toadstool. She bent to pick it up.

Prilla straightened, poured herself a steaming cup of tea, and –

"Hey!" she said. "Where did my other muffin go?"

Had she accidentally knocked it off the toadstool? She knelt down to look for it. But the missing strawberry muffin was nowhere to be found.

She stood and reached for her remaining muffin. But it was gone, too!

Prilla was puzzled. This was too odd. Pixie Hollow was a place of magic and whimsy. Strange things happened every day. But strawberry muffins didn't sprout legs and walk away. There had to be an explanation.

But try as she might, Prilla couldn't

come up with one. She poured herself a cup of tea. Then she settled down on the stone and took a sip. Her stomach rumbled again.

Looking around, Prilla spied a raspberry bush nearby. "I'll just have a berry for breakfast instead," she said.

Splat! A big juicy raspberry landed right on the toadstool table. Red juice splattered everywhere. Prilla jumped to her feet, spilling her tea. *Now, where did that come from?* She looked up at the sky. *A passing bird must have dropped it,* she thought.

"Lucky it didn't hit me on the head," she said out loud.

Splat!

Berry juice dripped down Prilla's face and onto the collar of her dress. She had spoken too soon!

She wiped the sticky juice from her forehead and cheeks with the cobweb napkin. *Unless I want every wasp in Pixie Hollow to be buzzing around me, I'd better get to Havendish Stream and wash this off*, she thought. She placed the cork back into the thermos, put the thermos in her sack, took a step forward – and promptly tripped on a pebble.

How odd, thought Prilla. *I didn't see that there before.*

Shrugging, she slung the sack over her shoulder and headed for Havendish Stream. "What a strange day," she said. "It would be funny if it weren't so... " Then she started to laugh despite herself. It *was* pretty funny that so many things had gone wrong!

Prilla got to the stream. She knelt on the bank, scooped up some of the clear, cool water, and splashed it on her face. She couldn't resist magically making a fountain or two spring up from the water when she had finished washing. *I'm getting pretty good at this,* she thought. *Rani would be proud.* Rani was the water-talent fairy who had taught Prilla how to make fountains. *Maybe she'll let me move on to water creatures next! I bet I could make a sea horse!*

Smiling at the idea, Prilla raised her head and began to straighten up. And there, on the opposite bank, sat a blue and golden butterfly. Prilla blinked. The butterfly fluttered its wings two or three times, then took off into the air.

Prilla was right behind it. She hoped

the butterfly would lead her straight to the rest of the herd.

She followed the butterfly along the banks of the stream. She trailed it through an underground passage. She chased it around and around a big oak tree until she was dizzy. She followed it past the Mermaid Lagoon... and ended up right back at Flower Field.

If I didn't know any better, Prilla thought, *I'd think this butterfly was taking me on a wild-goose chase!*

At the edge of Flower Field, the butterfly suddenly darted under a pile of dead leaves. Prilla landed nearby and slowly crept up to it. She stifled a giggle as she saw the leaves rustle. The silly butterfly thought it was fooling her!

Prilla lifted the top leaf.

This is a surprise! was all she could think.

For there was no butterfly under the leaf. Instead there was a Never stinkbug — an angry Never stinkbug. It *was* a surprise — and a particularly unpleasant one at that!

The stinkbug raised its tail, and — *whoosh!* — it drenched Prilla from head to toe in its horribly stinky perfume.

"Yuck!" cried Prilla. She stepped back, coughing.

As she wiped the tears from her eyes, she glanced up. Sitting on the branch above her head was the butterfly she had been chasing. Its wings were shaking. Prilla could have sworn that it was laughing at her.

9

THE BUTTERFLY FLEW OFF, but Prilla didn't follow. Instead, she sat down and put her head in her hands. She was stinky, sticky, and worn out. Maybe it was time to give up. It was quite clear to Prilla that she was a terrible butterfly herder. She had no idea what she was doing. She was starting to dislike butterfly herding – and butterflies themselves – very much.

Then again, if she gave up now, the herd might get lost, or harmed by predators. And it would all be her fault. Prilla couldn't bear the thought.

I can do this! she told herself. She stood up and began to retrace her steps.

When she returned to the spot where

her muffins had gone missing, to her surprise she spotted a butterfly. It was a pretty pink and bronze one. It sat there sunning itself on the toadstool she had used as a table.

The butterfly's back was to Prilla. Smiling, she slowly began to creep up behind it. She was careful not to step on a dead leaf or a twig. She didn't want to make any noise that would scare the butterfly away. *This is my last chance,* Prilla thought. She had to catch this butterfly!

Finally, Prilla was right behind the creature. She took a deep breath and lunged forward to grab it. "Gotcha!" she yelled.

The butterfly froze. Then it toppled over.

Prilla stared. Her mouth hung open

in disbelief. She reached over and softly poked the butterfly's wing with her finger. It didn't move.

No doubt about it. The butterfly was dead.

"What have I done?" Prilla cried. She took a deep breath. "Oh, why did I pretend to like butterflies in the first place?"

Once again there was a flash of purple, and Vidia landed right next to Prilla.

"Hello, precious," Vidia said with a smirk. "I've been looking for you all day. How's the butterfly herding going?" She wrinkled her nose. "And what is that awful smell? It smells like... ugh – stinkbug! Prilla, what in Never Land have you been up to?"

But Prilla was too upset to reply. She slowly raised her arm and pointed to the motionless butterfly.

Vidia looked at it, then turned to stare at Prilla. She wore a look of shock. "Precious, it's not... ?"

"Dead," finished Prilla forlornly. "Yes. I killed it!"

"My goodness, sweetheart," said Vidia. "Now you've really done it. Even *I've* never killed a butterfly."

This did not make Prilla feel any better. "I must have scared it to death," Prilla whispered.

Vidia shook her head. "You know, this never would have happened, darling, if you had just – "

Prilla put her hands over her ears. "I know, I know! But I can't think about that now. Will you please go get Queen Clarion so I can explain everything to her?"

Vidia raised an eyebrow. "Are you sure, dear?" she asked. "You could just pretend this never happened. I won't say a word."

Prilla was aghast. "No, Vidia! I must tell the queen."

"Suit yourself, precious," said Vidia. "I'll be back in two shakes of a dragon's tail."

Prilla watched as Vidia took off into the air. Then she lowered herself to the ground and leaned against the toadstool, where the tiny butterfly lay still. She could hardly stand to look at it. She closed her eyes and dropped her head into her hands. What a disaster this was!

She wasn't a butterfly-herding fairy. She was a butterfly-slaying fairy!

After what seemed like a lifetime, Prilla heard Vidia and Queen Clarion approach. She was surprised to see that Nettle was with them. *Maybe she's been brought along for an expert opinion,* Prilla thought. With all the butterfly herders sick, caterpillar-shearing-talent fairies were the next best thing.

Prilla wiped her eyes and stood up.

Nettle opened her mouth to say something. But Prilla held up her hand for silence. "Please let me speak," she said. "I have a confession to make, Queen Clarion. Something terrible has happened and it is all my fault."

"Go on, Prilla," said the queen.

"I... I.... I... killed a butterfly." Prilla lowered her eyes in shame.

"What butterfly? Where?" Queen Clarion asked sharply.

"Here," said Prilla, pointing to the toadstool. But when she turned her head to look, she was shocked.

The butterfly was gone!

10

"B-B-B-BUT IT WAS JUST HERE a minute ago," Prilla stuttered. She turned to Vidia. "You saw it. Tell her!"

Vidia gave her a wicked smile, which made Prilla even more upset. She turned to the queen. "It's true! It was just there!"

"What did the butterfly look like?" the queen asked.

"It was pink and bronze," Prilla said. She was trying hard not to cry. "It was very small... "

The queen burst out laughing. "Perhaps it looks like the butterfly that is sitting on your head?" she asked.

Nettle started laughing, too. Vidia shook her head, smirking.

Could it be true? Prilla reached up. Sure enough, there was a butterfly sitting on her head like a jaunty little hat! It took off into the air and landed on the toadstool. It was the very same butterfly Prilla thought she had startled to death.

"But how… ?" Prilla began.

"Oh, Prilla," said Nettle, catching her breath. "Don't you know that butterflies like to play practical jokes?"

"What are you talking about?" said Prilla.

"They'll do anything to play a trick on you," Nettle explained. "One time a butterfly carried away my best pair of shears. And the next morning, all the caterpillars had terrible haircuts!"

"And there was that time a herd of butterflies picked up a sparrow man who had fallen asleep in a patch of clover," Queen Clarion added. "They took him to one of the highest branches of the Home Tree. He was horribly confused when he woke up later, high above the ground."

"But this is the meanest butterfly trick I've ever seen," Nettle told Prilla. "Imagine, it pretended to be dead so you'd think you had killed it."

"It *was* a good joke," Vidia said. She liked mean jokes.

Prilla stared at the other fairies. She couldn't believe what she was hearing. "That can't be right," she said. But then she started thinking about the day's events. Getting stuck on the twig. Having her hands tied up with spider silk. The sneezewort. The missing muffins. The berry that fell on her head. Tripping over the pebble. The stinkbug attack. And this – the butterfly that played dead.

"I can't believe it! So *that's* what's been going on all day," said Prilla. She was so relieved, she started to chuckle.

Nettle and the queen gave her puzzled looks. "But you love butterflies. So why didn't you know about them?" Nettle finally asked.

Prilla stopped laughing. It was time to tell the truth. "I–I–I told a lie," she admitted. She was too ashamed to make eye contact with anyone. She stared at her shoes as she spoke. "I said that I liked butterflies. But the truth was that I didn't really like them at all. And I didn't know a single thing about herding them. I still don't!"

"But why did you say you liked

butterflies?" the queen asked.

Prilla gulped. She began to explain how at first she had felt honoured when other fairies asked her to help out with their talents. And how, after a while, it had begun to take time away from her own talent. But she had been afraid to say no to the fairies who needed her.

Prilla turned to her friend. "Nettle, to be honest, I don't really like shearing caterpillars. I'd rather blink over to the mainland. I didn't want to hurt your feelings, so I pretended that I liked butterflies."

"Prilla," said Nettle, "you silly fairy. I love my talent. I think you're crazy for not liking it, too. But I would never want you to do something you didn't like."

"Yes," said the queen. "Prilla, you

can be an honorary whatever-you-like talent in your spare time. But Pixie Hollow has only one mainland-visiting clapping-talent fairy, and we need you."

Vidia snorted. "Imagine liking butterflies! Didn't you think something was odd when no one else would volunteer?"

"Not even animal-talent fairies like working with butterflies!" Nettle added. "They're one of the only creatures they can't communicate with."

Prilla nodded. She felt embarrassed and happy and relieved all at once. Then she noticed that the pink and bronze butterfly had landed by her feet. She looked at it affectionately. Sure, the butterflies had made her life difficult. But they were beautiful creatures. And they

The Full Moon Fairy Dance

When the moon is full, there's only one place in *Never Land* to be – the Fairy Dance in *Pixie Hollow*!

Bathed in silver light from the full moon, the Never Fairies gather in the Fairy Circle to dance the night away with their friends.

The *Full Moon Fairy Dance* is the highlight of the month for every Never Fairy! It's a chance to show off new outfits, catch up with friends, eat **scrumptious** banquets and dance the *magical fairy dance*.

With this **essential** guide to the Full Moon Dance, the power of your imagination and a sprinkle of pixie dust, you can be there too!

And remember… **believing is just the beginning!**

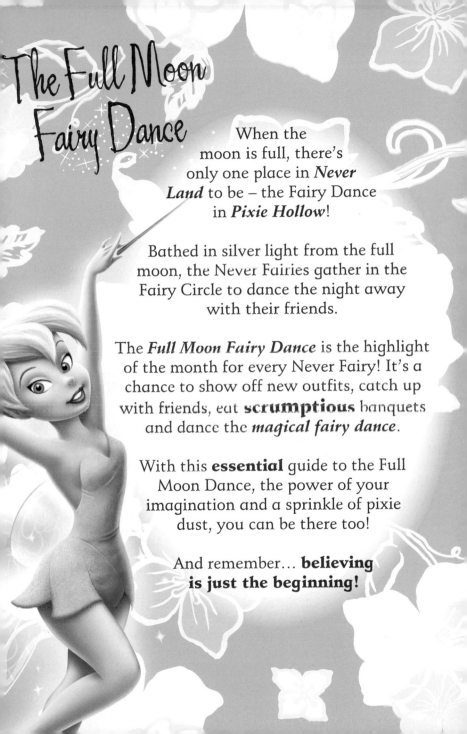

Socialising

As a soft breeze blows through the Never trees and flowers, it carries the delightful sound of fairy **laughter** - and it's coming from the Fairy Circle! The echoes of fairy gossip are also carried on the wind, although not all fairies like gossip – especially *Tink*, she hates gossip!

If you follow the sound of the *cheeky* fairy voices then you'll find the Full Moon Dance. It's a very special occasion and only happens once a month – when the moon is full in the night's sky.

The Full Moon Dance gives fairies a chance to catch up with friends from different talent groups, who they might not get a chance to talk to at other times. Garden Fairies can pass on weeding tips to Water Fairies and Light Fairies can **dazzle** their Tinkering friends with new light displays.

This **magical** night is an important event in a Never Fairy's social calendar. The enchantment of fairy laughter and dancing is very powerful though, and an extra helping of *pixie dust* is required before each fairy attends the dance.

Remember, a fairy circle is the name of where the gathering is held but that doesn't mean that Tink and her friends will be standing in a circle all night. Fairies gather in many shapes including squares, triangles, untidy clumps, hovering clouds and even pyramids!

Fairy Food

Never Fairies **love** to eat! And the Fairy Dance every full moon is a perfect excuse for a banquet. Besides, it's important to keep up a fairy's energy when there's so much **dancing** to be done!

In between dances, the fairies will sit down together to enjoy **scrumptious** dishes that have been prepared by the baking-talent fairies. The Full Moon Banquet is a perfect opportunity for fairies to sit down and catch up with one another – in fact; sitting around a banqueting table is as much about socialising as it is about **eating!**

There is such an **enormous** selection of fairy food on offer at every banquet that a fairy is often spoilt for choice! Each dish is perfectly formed and tastes **sublime.**

This is an example of a Full Moon Banquet menu...

To start...

Acorn Soup with a poppy-puff roll

*

Dwarf mushroom caps filled with sesame seed purée

Main course...

Roasted mock turtle with chestnut dumplings and cherry sauce

Sweet...

Strawberry angel food cake with nutmeg sprinkles

*

Barley cracker with mouse brie

*

Warm Buttermilk with star-shaped butter cookies

Music and Dancing

The are lots of music-talent fairies in Pixie
Hollow and these **sassy** pixies provide the
musical accompaniment for the dance. Pipes
and flutes are carved from the bark of a
Bimbim tree. Drums are made from leaves
stretched over acorn caps and harps are
strung together from finely spun spider silk.

Never Fairies have *beautiful* singing voices and
love the fact that the Full Moon Dance gives
them the chance to all sing together – the
sound of **hundreds** of fairies singing is
utterly **mesmerising!**

Favourite songs include:
"Fairy Dust Melody" – this is Mother Dove's
favourite song.
"Fly Not Far from Me" – this is the fairies'
saddest song and is often played at the end
of the fairy dance.

After feasting, storytelling, chatting and comparing outfits, the fairies form a ring and get ready to dance the *Fairy Dance!*

This is the favourite part of the evening for many fairies; they even spend time rehearsing the dance steps in preparation for the **big** event!

Tinker Bell and her fairy friends love to perform the Fairy Dance! The dance itself is a complicated airborne dance, which involves fluid movements of wings, legs, arms and heads. It's beautiful to watch but could send any non-fairy into a trance, as the magic is so **powerful.** Therefore be careful if you should ever catch a glimpse!

But it's easy to imagine what the dance must look like – it's **magical** and *beautiful* – just like the fairies themselves.

Take the Fairy Dance Test!

Other than the magical Fairy Dance, many other types of dances are performed over the full moon. Take the test below to find out which dance would suit you best.

1. **What kind of outfit would you like to wear to a dance?**
A. A short skirt and a tank-top
B. A long frilly skirt and a large hat
C. Something that sparkles under disco lights
D. Leggings and a funky top

2. **What sort of music do you like to dance to?**
A. Rock music
B. Anything that's fun and really loud
C. Electronic dance music
D. Swingin' piano music

3. **What's your favourite dance move?**
A. Anything involving fancy footwork
B. High kicks
C. The Hustle
D. Hand jiving

Answers:
• *If you scored mostly As then the Fairy Boogie-Woogie is the dance for you. You're sassy and funny!*
• *If you scored mostly Bs then the Fairy Cancan is the dance for you. You're outgoing and love to spend time with others!*
• *If you scored mostly Cs then the Fairy Disco Dance is the dance for you. You've got cutting-edge style!*
• *If you scored mostly Ds then the Fairy Jive is the dance for you. You know how to have a good time!*

really didn't mean any harm; they were just... mischievous.

Perhaps she didn't hate butterflies after all.

Prilla took a step towards the butterfly. Immediately, she sprawled out on the ground. The sneaky little butterfly had tied her shoelaces together!

There was a moment of embarrassed silence. Then Prilla started laughing. Queen Clarion and Nettle joined in. Vidia crossed her arms and gave Prilla a mocking look.

And the butterfly? It was laughing, too, of course!

No, Prilla thought, shaking her head. *I definitely do not like butterflies one bit, that is for sure!*

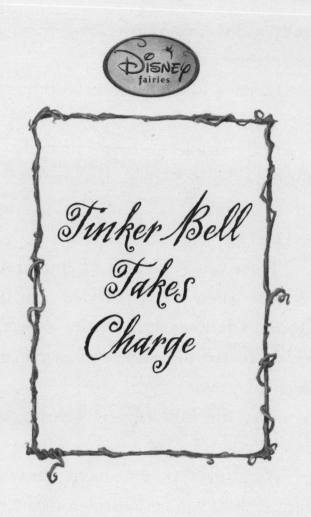

Tinker Bell
Takes
Charge

1

IT WAS A MILD, sunny day in Pixie Hollow—a perfect sort of a day. Little white clouds scampered across a dazzling blue sky. A soft breeze rustled the leaves of the Home Tree, the great ageless maple where the Never fairies lived.

Although it was a perfect day, Tinker Bell was not in her usual high spirits. Something was bothering her, but she could not figure out what it was. She wasn't sick. She wasn't sad. It was more like she had an itch that she couldn't find, let alone scratch.

Just that morning, she had caught sight of her face in the polished walls of the Home Tree's lobby. She'd noticed her slumped shoulders and the frown on her face. Even her ponytail drooped.

This troublesome feeling was on her mind now as she flew towards her bedroom, which was high in the branches of the Home Tree. She needed to change her shoes before she could go back to her workshop. The ones she was wearing had been soaked on a visit to Thistle's strawberry patch. Thistle, a garden-talent fairy, had asked Tink to look at a garden hoe that needed fixing. It had been left on the damp ground

among the strawberries, and the blade
had rusted through. It would have to
be replaced. *But it will be easy to fix,*
Tink thought.

She headed up through the trunk
of the Home Tree. The trunk split into
branches. She turned right, then left, then
left again, winding upwards. The corridor
narrowed as the tree's limbs tapered.

Tink's bedroom was at the end of
one of the topmost branches. When the
hallway was so tight that her head nearly
grazed the ceiling, she reached the door
to her room.

As soon as she was inside, her spirits
lifted a bit. Tink loved her room.
Everything in it reflected her talent and
personality. There was her beloved bed,
which was made from a pirate's metal

loaf pan. There were the lampshades made from old colanders. Even the chair she was sitting on was special. The back of it was made from a serving platter, the seat was a frying pan, and the legs were made from old serving spoons.

At one point or another, Tink had repaired the frying pan, the platter, and each of the spoons. Some she had repaired more than once. But eventually, pans and spoons wore out. Although Tink thought anything broken could be fixed, the kitchen-talent fairies didn't always agree. Sometimes they threw their worn-out pots and platters away.

Tink felt a special connection with every pot and pan she'd ever fixed. She couldn't bear to see any of them on the scrap-metal heap. So when the kitchen-talent fairies had thrown out the pan, the platter, and the spoons, she'd rescued them and brought them back to her workshop. With a lot of thought and a few pinches of fairy dust, she'd turned them into a chair.

Tink thought about the frying-pan chair as she closed the door to her room and flew back down through the Home Tree. What a wonderful challenge it had been to make. Not like fixing Thistle's silly rusted hoe. There was no challenge at all in that.

Suddenly Tink stopped in her tracks.

"That's it!" she said aloud. "That is what's bothering me! No challenge!"

Tink was one of the best pots-and-pans-talent fairies in all of Pixie Hollow.

Her joy came from fixing things. She liked a challenging problem more than almost anything.

But for weeks now, every job Tink had been given had been as easy as apple pie. No pots that wouldn't boil water. No colanders that refused to drain. No pans that were more hole than pan. Just "fix this little hole, fix that little hole." Boring, boring, boring.

But at least now I know what's wrong, Tink thought. *What I need is a problem to solve! A big one!*

"Tink!" A voice behind her interrupted her thoughts. Tink turned. Her good friend Rani, a water-talent fairy, was hurrying towards her.

Being the only fairy without wings, Rani could not fly. So Tink gently landed on the moss carpet in the Home Tree's hallway. She waited until Rani caught up.

"Where are you going?" Rani asked.

"I was just on my way back to my workshop," Tink replied. "Why do you – "

"Ask?" said Rani. She had a habit of finishing everyone's sentences. "No big reason. I just thought maybe we could play a game of – "

But Rani never got to finish. At that moment, she was interrupted by a tremendous crash. Both fairies heard branches cracking and snapping near the top of the Home Tree.

In the next instant, there was a *thud* that shook the tree to its very roots. Tink and Rani nearly lost their balance. From the nearby tearoom came the sound of dishes falling and shattering.

Then there was silence.

Tink and Rani stared at each other.

"Did the moon just fall out of the sky?" Rani whispered in awe.

"Maybe it was a branch falling from another tree," said Tink. But even as she spoke, she knew that wasn't it. The sound had been made by something very heavy and solid. And it had landed quite close by.

The two fairies listened carefully. After a long moment Tink took a deep breath and straightened her shoulders. "We've got to go and see – "

"What it is. If you say so," said Rani. She dabbed her forehead with a leafkerchief and attempted to smile bravely. Though they were both nervous, it was a lot easier to see it on Rani. She was the most watery of all the water-talent fairies. At the moment, her forehead was beaded with sweat.

The two fairies headed back towards the front entrance of the Home Tree. Tink walked so that she wouldn't get too far ahead of Rani. Brave as she was, even Tink didn't want to go outside alone. Together they hurried past the tearoom, down the corridor, through the entrance hall and out the knothole door.

When Tink stepped into the sunlight, she stopped cold and gasped. Rani, who was right on Tink's heels, crashed into her.

Rani peeked over Tink's shoulder. She gasped, too.

"*What* is *that?*" she whispered.

2

RIGHT IN FRONT of them was a huge, menacing-looking black ball. It was taller than two fairies put together and just as wide. It had landed right in the middle of the Home Tree's courtyard.

A large crack ran through the courtyard where it had smashed down. Several toadstool chairs had been damaged or squashed completely. The ground around the ball was covered with the splintered remains of branches and twigs.

Tink's mind reeled. The courtyard was a very special place for the fairies. Many of their most important meetings and celebrations were held there. Not to mention, the fairies had to fly through it to reach the Home Tree's knothole door.

Whenever Tink saw the courtyard, she felt that she was home. It always seemed to say, "Welcome. The Home Tree waits to embrace you." Now the sight of the damaged courtyard made her heart ache.

A large crowd of fairies had gathered around the ball. Clarion, the fairy queen, stepped forward.

"Is everyone all right?" she asked. Her voice was tense with worry. "Is anyone hurt?"

Noses and wings were quickly counted, amid a buzz of concern. Incredibly, every fairy in the Home Tree had escaped harm.

The queen sighed with relief. She looked around the crowd. "Terence,

Spring, Jerome, Rosetta, Luna," she said. Her voice had regained its normal regal tone. The fairies and sparrow men sprang to attention. "Fly to the top of the tree and see what damage has been done. Please report back at once."

With Terence, a fairy-dust-talent sparrow man, in the lead, the group took off.

When they had gone, a scullery-talent fairy tiptoed up to the great ball. She raised her hand as if to touch its rough surface. But at the last second she pulled her hand back. "Do you think it might be alive?" she whispered.

All at once, the fairies nearest to the ball hopped back a couple of steps.

"What's it made of?" asked Dulcie, a baking-talent fairy.

The fairies around her shook their heads, muttering, "Don't know."

"Maybe it's a big rock," said Angus, a pots-and-pans-talent sparrow man. "Though I've certainly never seen a rock this round before."

"Maybe it's a giant black pearl," said Rani. "Though I've never seen a pearl this big."

Tink shook her head. "No," she said. "It would be shiny if it were a pearl."

Dulcie flew hesitantly up to it. She gave it a small rap with her knuckles. "Ow!" she said. "It's hard!" She blew on her hand. "And it's hot!" she added.

Tink didn't like to stand around. And she had stood around long enough. Bravely, she marched up to the ball and gave it a good hard smack.

"It's iron," she said. She shook her hand to cool it off from the hot metal. "Good old-fashioned Never iron."

Several fairies frowned. "Iron is really heavy," Dulcie said worriedly.

"It's going to be hard to move," said Rani. She started to cry.

"We should try to find out where it came from," the queen told them. "That might help us figure out how to get rid of it."

Her suggestion was greeted with enthusiasm. "Let's take a good look at it," said Rani. She wiped the tears from her eyes.

The fairies all moved in closer. They circled the ball. Some fairies flew around the top. Others bent down low to look at the part that touched the ground.

"Hold on!" said Tink. She hovered like a hummingbird near the very top of the ball. "I see something."

Other fairies flew over to join her. "You're right," said Lily, a garden-talent fairy. "It's some kind of a mark."

Angus nodded. "It's almost like a – "

"A hook!" Tink shouted in triumph. "It's a mark that looks like a hook! And you know what that means."

"*Captain Hook!*" cried several fairies.

"Of course. Why didn't I realise it before? It's a cannonball!" Tink declared.

Tink had seen plenty of cannonballs back in the days when she had spent all her time with Peter Pan. But she had never before seen a cannonball in Pixie Hollow. Hook and his pirates never came to this part of Never Land's forest. And the fairies tried to avoid the pirates as much as they could.

Just then, they heard a muffled boom from the direction of Pirate Cove. Several fairies jumped.

"Cannon fire," said Queen Clarion. "Captain Hook must be after Peter Pan again."

The others knew what she meant. On Never Land, there was an on-and-off battle between Hook and his pirates and Peter and the Lost Boys. On certain quiet nights, when the wind was just right, the fairies could hear Pan and Hook's swords clashing in the distance.

"Hmm," said Tink with a worried little frown. Peter Pan was a friend of Tink's. Though she rarely saw him anymore, she knew him better than any of the other fairies did. She didn't like to think of Captain Hook firing cannonballs at Peter.

But Peter is too quick and too clever to get hit by a cannonball, Tink assured herself.

There was another muffled boom, followed by a whizzing sound.

"Everyone, duck!" said the queen.

The fairies all dashed for cover in the roots of the Home Tree. Something flew through the air high over their heads. It landed in the nearby forest with a tremendous thud.

"The fairy circle!" cried Dulcie. She

hurried out from behind a root. "What if it landed there?"

"What about Mother Dove?" Rani said, almost in a whisper. "What if it hit her hawthorn tree?"

The fairies looked at each other in stricken silence. Mother Dove was the closest thing to pure goodness in all of Never Land. She was the source of all the fairies' magic. They had almost lost her once, when a hurricane hit Never Land. The thought of losing her again was too dreadful to bear.

In a tense voice, Queen Clarion told several fast-flying fairies to fly to the hawthorn and check on Mother Dove. They zipped off in a blur.

Moments later, the fast fliers were back.

"Mother Dove is fine," a fast-flying sparrow man reported. "Not one feather ruffled. And the fairy circle is undamaged."

The fairies let out a collective sigh of relief.

Tink glared at the big black cannonball in the courtyard. "How dare those pirates!" she exclaimed. "How could they be so careless? I say – "

But before she could say more, Spring, a message-talent fairy, came speeding up to her. She had a grim look on her face.

"Tink," she said. "I've just been to the top of the Home Tree. I think you'd better come with me."

3

WHAT NOW? Tink wondered. *And what does it have to do with me?*

Maybe something metal has broken, and they need me to fix it, Tink mused. *But why right at this moment?*

She followed the messenger into the Home Tree. They passed through the main corridor, where paintings representing each different Never fairy talent hung on the walls. Tink saw that most of the paintings were crooked. Some had even fallen to the floor. She stopped and straightened the painting of a dented stewpot, which was the symbol for the pots-and-pans talent.

Up through the branches they went. They turned right, then left, then left again. Finally, they came to the corridor that led to Tink's room. Tink saw her friend Terence waiting for her. Terence had been in the group the queen had sent to check the damage to the tree. He looked upset.

"Tink," he said, "I hardly know how to tell you this. Your bedroom – "

Her beloved bedroom! Tink didn't even wait for him to finish his sentence. She zoomed down the corridor to the end of the branch where her room sat. What would she find? she wondered. Would it be a horrible mess? Would her loaf-pan bed be overturned, or even dented? It was not a pleasant thought.

When she reached the tip of the branch, she stopped cold.

Her room wasn't a mess. Her room

wasn't there at all.

Tinker Bell hovered, staring. The walls, the ceiling, and everything in the room had disappeared. All that remained was the floor and the jagged edges of the broken walls.

She looked up past the hole where her ceiling should have been. The surrounding branches had a few broken twigs. But the other fairies' rooms were still there. The cannonball had hit Tink's room, and Tink's alone.

Tink felt faint. She sat down cross-legged on the floor.

How could my room just be... gone? she thought. *Where will I sleep? Where will I keep my clothes and other things? Where* are *my clothes and other things?*

More fairies began to arrive to see

what had happened.

"Oh, Tink," said her friend Beck. "It's awful!"

"I can't believe it," said Prilla. "Your bed is gone. And it was such a great bed."

Tink stood up. She didn't want the other fairies to feel sorry for her. She took a deep breath. "We'll just rebuild it," she said. She sounded calmer than she felt. "And it will be an even better room than before."

"We'll all help you," said Terence. The others nodded in agreement.

Suddenly Tink felt angry. After all, no one would have to rebuild anything if it weren't for the cannonball. Her hands balled into tiny fists thinking about it.

"And in the meantime," she said

fiercely, "we're going to get that horrid cannonball out of our courtyard. What do you say, fairies?"

"Yes!" they all cried. "Let's do it!" With Tink in the lead, the fairies went back to the courtyard. The most obvious thing was to try pushing the cannonball, Tink decided. "If a lot of us get behind it and fly as hard as we can, maybe we can roll it out of the courtyard," she said.

"Let's move every little twig out of its path. That way it won't get stuck on anything," said Beck.

The cleaning-talent fairies grabbed their brooms and swept up all the splinters. Other fairies helped by moving the pieces of the squashed mushroom chairs.

"All right," said Tink. "Let's get into pushing formation."

Several fairies arranged themselves behind the ball. The strongest ones hovered close to the bottom. The weaker ones stayed near the top.

"One, two, three... *shove!*" shouted Tink.

The fairies beat their wings madly. They heaved against the ball as hard as they could.

After a moment, they stopped. Several fairies leaned against the ball, panting.

"I think it moved a tiny, tiny bit," said Prilla, who was inclined to see the best in all situations.

"It didn't move an inch," said Angus, who was not.

"Let's give it another try," said Tink.

They rearranged themselves. Now the strongest fairies went to the top of the ball. The weaker ones went to the bottom.

"One, two, three... *shove!*" Tink cried again.

The fairies used every ounce of strength they had. At last they stopped. Their wings were quivering with exhaustion.

"Nothing," said Angus.

Indeed, the ball had not moved, not a hair.

Tink sighed. "Well, I guess that's not going to work," she said. "But this is only the beginning."

4

AS THE OTHER FAIRIES sat down to rest, Tink began to pace. She was sure she could come up with an idea that would work. She tugged at her fringe, thinking hard.

Down in the meadow near the dairy barn, the faint sound of bells could be heard. Cannonball or no cannonball, the dairy mice had to be fed. The mouse-herding-talent fairies were taking the herd out to pasture.

Tink looked towards the meadow. "Mice!" she said suddenly.

"Mice?" said two of the fairies nearest to her.

"Yes," said Tink. "Mice. It's simple. We'll harness all the dairy mice to the cannonball. Maybe, together, all of them can move it!"

"Wonderful idea, Tink!" said Queen Clarion.

The messenger-talent fairies headed for the pasture to tell the mouse-herding fairies to round up the dairy mice. Meanwhile, the kitchen-talent fairies hurried back to the kitchen to collect all the loaves of acorn bread they could spare. The mice adored acorn bread. Occasionally, a mouse would get loose from the herd and be caught in the Home Tree pantry, nibbling bread. Now the fairies could use the bread as a lure to get the mice to pull the ball.

Fairies from other talents pitched in too. Florian and the rest of the weaving-talent fairies quickly fashioned ropes from sweet grass they'd plucked from the meadow.

"I wish we had time to collect marsh grass," Florian said. "It makes a stronger rope. But I think this should do."

It only took a few minutes for the mouse-herders to get the mice to the Home Tree. One by one, the fairies began to harness the mice to the rope. Altogether, there were thirty-six mice. They stood to attention, their noses quivering.

At last, they were all in formation. The mouse-herding fairies stood just in front of them, waving the bread. The mice squeaked excitedly at the sight and smell of it.

"That's it, my little loves," said one of the mouse herders. "Delicious bread!

Come and get it."

She stepped back a little. The mice strained towards her. "Come on," the fairy urged. "Acorn bread! More than you've ever had before. You can have it all if you just try!"

And the mice did try. They loved that bread more than anything, much more than the sweetgrass seeds they were usually fed. They strained towards the bread. Their little claws dug into the ground. The courtyard echoed with the sounds of their squeaking.

The other fairies cheered them on. "You can do it, mice!" they yelled. "Get the bread! Move the ball! You can do it!"

The ball wobbled. The mice leaned into their harnesses – and the ball moved. Not a lot, maybe half an inch. But it moved.

"It's working, Tink!" cried Terence. He gave her an enormous smile and clapped her on the back.

"It's working! It's working!" other fairies echoed.

Tink's face was flushed. Her eyes shone. All her attention was focused on the cannonball. It moved another half inch, and

Snap!

The rope around the cannonball broke. The mice leaped forward, suddenly free from the weight. They lunged at the bread in the mouse-herders' hands and quickly began to gobble it down.

The fairies stopped in mid-cheer. Everyone let out a disappointed sigh.

"Marsh grass," said Florian. She shook her head. "It always makes a stronger rope."

Tink flew over to look at the mice. They were still panting from the effort of pulling the ball. Their furry sides heaved in and out.

"Do you think they could do it again?" she asked one of the mouse-herding fairies. "If we made a stronger rope, that is."

The fairy shook her head. "I don't think so," she said. "It might wear them out. Dairy mice can be quite delicate, you know. If they get too tired, they stop giving milk."

Tink's shoulders slumped. But she tried hard not to show her disappointment. "Well," she said, "it was a good try. We'll just have to think of something else."

Queen Clarion spoke up. "Maybe that's enough work for one day," she said gently. "The cannonball won't go anywhere before tomorrow. Why don't we all get cleaned up and have some dinner?"

The fairies murmured their agreement. Not only were they all tired, they were also very hungry.

As the other fairies headed into the Home Tree, Tink lingered behind.

Well, Tink, you wanted a challenge, she said to herself. *And now you've got one.*

She stared up at the huge cannonball. *But am I up to it?* she wondered.

5

BECAUSE THE KITCHEN was such a mess, dinner that night was simple – acorn-butter sandwiches with dandelion salad. The tired fairies ate quickly. The sun had already set. After a long, hard day of work, they were eager to go to bed.

As soon as she had eaten, Tink realised she had a problem. She had nowhere to sleep. She watched as the other fairies headed for their rooms. In all the excitement over the cannonball, they had forgotten that Tink didn't have her own room to go to.

The tearoom slowly emptied. Tink remained sitting at her table. She wasn't sure what to do. As the shadows lengthened, she felt more and more forlorn.

At last Rani noticed Tink sitting alone. She realised the problem at once.

"Tink," she said, "what will you do tonight?"

"I think maybe I'll just sleep outside," Tink replied bravely. "I can use a maple leaf as a blanket."

"You can sleep in my room," Rani told her. "It's better than sleeping outside, anyway."

"Okay," Tink said. She felt relieved. "I would like that. I'm awfully tired."

Tink followed Rani up to her room. She had visited Rani's room many times before. But until that evening, she hadn't noticed the details. She looked around at the blue-green walls and the seaweed curtains hanging in the windows. The floor was paved with smooth river stones.

It seemed like a quiet, peaceful place. Tink was looking forward to a good night's sleep.

"I think I'm ready to go to bed." yawned Tink. "Where should I sleep?"

"I could pile lots of blankets on the floor." Rani suggested.

"Let me help you," said Tink.

Together, they piled woven-fern blankets on the floor until they had made a soft bed.

"That should be very comfortable," Tink said when they had finished. But she could not help noticing how humid Rani's room was. Even the blankets felt damp.

Tink settled herself on the pile. She was so tired, she was sure she'd fall asleep in a moment.

Rani covered her up with a sheet, which was also slightly damp. "Good night, dear friend," she said. Then she climbed into her own bed, which was made from driftwood. She pulled the seaweed quilt up to her chin.

Tink lay on her back, gazing at the blue-green ceiling. *It was nice of Rani to take me in*, she thought. Then she closed her eyes and gave in to her tiredness.

Seconds later, Tink opened her eyes. She could feel a lump beneath the pile of blankets. It was one of the river stones that paved the floor.

Tink tried turning on her side, but that was no better. She flopped over on her stomach, but that was even worse. She ended up on her back again.

Tink thought wistfully of her comfy loaf-pan bed and the soft, dappled light that came through the colander lampshades in her room. How she loved to fall asleep beneath the still life of the stockpot, whisk, and griddle. And now it was gone, all gone. Tink sighed.

Moonlight filtered in through the seaweed curtains. Suddenly Tink gasped and jumped up. Two long arms seemed to reach out to her from the corner of the room.

Rani heard her and sat straight up. "What's the matter?" she cried.

"Th-there's something in the corner!" whispered Tink. She was almost too scared to breathe.

"Where? I don't see it!" whispered Rani. She followed the direction of Tink's pointing finger. But the room was too dark. They couldn't see clearly.

Quickly, Rani lit her scallop-shell lamp. Then she started to giggle. "That's just my clothes hanging on a clothes tree, Tink. It's made from a coral branch. Remember?"

Gradually, Tink's heart stopped racing. Her breath returned to normal. "Oh," she said. "So it is." Now she felt foolish. She wished more than ever that she could be in her own bed.

Rani turned out the light. They settled back down to sleep.

Tink tried to drift off, she really did. But the paving rocks were not getting any softer. And then she became aware of another thing.

Drip. Drip. Drip-drip. Drip.

It was a slow, steady rhythm. Tink had forgotten all about Rani's drip. She had a permanent leak in her room, whether it was raining or not. Beneath the leak sat a bucket made from a human-sized thimble. Inside the bucket, a Never minnow swam contentedly around and around.

Drip. Drip. Drip-drip. Drip.

By now, Tink had given up trying to sleep. She lay on her back and stared at the ceiling. Every now and then she shifted her wings under the damp sheet to find a better position.

Sometime before dawn, Tink heard a new noise. It was Rani crying.

"Rani," whispered Tink, "are you

all right?"

There was no answer, just more crying. Tink brightened her glow so she could see Rani a little better. Rani was sound asleep, weeping onto her pillow. The air in the room was getting damper and damper.

"Rani," Tink tried again. "Wake up. You're having a bad dream."

Still Rani did not wake. Tink finally gave up and went back to staring at the ceiling. She listened to the dripping water and Rani's crying.

A little after dawn, Rani awoke. She sat up in bed and stretched her arms towards the ceiling. "I just had the most wonderful dream!" she said when she saw that Tink was awake.

"No, you didn't. You had an awful

dream," Tink snapped. She was fairly cross, having not slept a wink the whole night.

Rani gave her a strange look and shook her head. "No, it was long and wonderful," she said. "I was playing with a big ball of water. I was tossing it back and forth with Silvermist and Tally. We could throw it as high as the top of the Home Tree and make a rainbow in the sunlight. It was so beautiful!"

Now it was Tink's turn to give Rani a strange look. "But you were crying," she insisted. "Cupfuls. Buckets. Barrels. Feel your bed, it's all – "

Rani broke into a big grin. " – wet," she finished. "I was crying in the dream, too! Crying from happiness!"

Tink just shook her head. She got

up from her damp, lumpy bed. "Rani," she said, "you are my very good friend. But I am a pots-and-pans fairy and you are a water fairy, and I will never truly understand you." She smiled and gave Rani a hug.

Rani's eyes filled with tears again. "You're my good friend, too. And I'll never really understand you, either," she said, hugging Tink back. She wiped her eyes with a leafkerchief. "Do you want to go have some breakfast?"

"Yes," said Tink. "But my wings are too damp to fly."

Rani picked up another leafkerchief and gently dried Tink's wings. Then they went downstairs for breakfast.

6

BREAKFAST WAS VERY GOOD, as usual. Platters of Dulcie's wonderful pumpkin muffins and pots of blackberry tea sat on every table in the tearoom. But no breakfast would have been delicious enough to cheer Tink up that morning.

Tink was tired. She was damp. And she wanted her room back.

She stared gloomily at the serving platter in front of her. It reminded her of her platter–frying-pan–spoon chair.

"Rough night?" asked Angus. He was sitting next to Tink at the pots-and-pans-talent table.

"Just a little damp," said Tink with a sigh. She took a sip of tea. "But don't worry. I'm ready to get to work. I'll have that cannonball out of Pixie Hollow in no time." Even to her own ears, she did not sound very sure.

"Tinker Bell!" a cheerful voice exclaimed. Tink turned around. Gwinn, a tiny decoration-talent fairy, was beaming at her. "Are you ready to start putting your room back together?" Gwinn asked. "Cedar and I are heading up there now to get started." She gestured at Cedar, who was standing behind her.

Cedar was the biggest, strongest-looking fairy Tinker Bell had ever seen. She was nearly six inches tall! It was clear from the hammer and saw Cedar was carrying that she was a carpenter-talent fairy.

Cedar nodded shyly in greeting.

Her great height made Gwinn look even tinier.

"Usually, we prepare rooms for fairies who have just arrived in Never Land," Gwinn continued. She spoke very, very fast. Tink had to concentrate to keep up. "Of course, we don't know them yet. So we just make our best guess about what that fairy might want. And then we hope she likes it. But you're already *here!* I've never helped a fairy decorate her own room before! You can tell me exactly what you want! It will be perfect! *Perfect!* Right, Cedar?"

Cedar nodded and stared bashfully at the ground.

Tink bit her lip. She wanted to start rebuilding her room. But she had promised to get rid of the cannonball.

Angus read her mind. "You can work on the cannonball later, Tink, after you and Gwinn decide what your new room should look like," he pointed out.

Tink thought about it for a moment. Angus was right. The cannonball could wait.

"All right," Tink said. She smiled. "Let's go!"

A short time later, Tink was watching Cedar hammer planks into the walls of her new room.

Gwinn flew from one corner to the next, measuring the space with her eyes. She kept up a steady stream of chatter.

"You'll want silver paint," Gwinn told Tink. "Or maybe gold. Or something copper? Ooh, yes! Copper could be just lovely with the sunlight coming in – "

"Silver will be fine," said Tink, trying to keep up.

"And I suppose you'd like colander lampshades again," Gwinn went on. "Although a nice iris-petal lantern would give the room a softer look… "

"Colanders, please," Tink cut in. She was surprised to find she was having fun.

"And you'll need curtains, a bedspread, some kind of rug… " Gwinn zipped from corner to corner. She was making Tink dizzy.

Tink sat down in the middle of the bare floor to watch her.

Gwinn will make sure that the walls are the right colour, Tink thought. *And she will get new colanders for the lamps.* But Gwinn couldn't make her another still life painting. And Cedar couldn't make her another loaf-pan bed.

If I want my room back just the way it was, Tink thought, *I'm going to have to take matters into my own hands.*

"I'll be back in a little while," she told Gwinn and Cedar.

Cedar mumbled goodbye through a mouthful of nails. Gwinn absent-mindedly waved some curtain fabric at her. Tink flew out through the open ceiling and over the woods of Pixie Hollow.

Soon, Tink arrived at Bess's studio. It was made from an old tangerine crate that the art-talent fairy had set up in a remote clearing in the woods, where she could paint in peace and quiet.

Tink found Bess hard at work. She

was painting a portrait of an animal-talent fairy. The animal-talent fairy posed on a cushion, holding her favourite ladybird on her lap.

"Tink!" Bess said. She set down her brush and hugged her friend. "What a terrible thing to happen to your room. Is there anything I can do to help?"

"Actually, there is," said Tink. She explained that she needed another still life of a stockpot, whisk, and griddle to hang over her bed.

Bess looked a little embarrassed. "Oh, Tink," she said unhappily. "Of *course* I'll paint a new picture for you. But I won't be able to get to it for a while. I've already promised paintings to five other fairies."

The animal-talent fairy cleared her

throat impatiently. The ladybird on her lap was getting restless. Bess gave Tink another hug, and then got back to work.

Tink flew off, trying not to feel discouraged. Her next stop was the kitchen. She hoped to find some pots and pans that were beyond repair. With luck, she could make another frying-pan chair exactly like her old one.

Dulcie met Tink at the kitchen door. She was carrying a tray of pretty little tea cakes. As Dulcie set the cakes on a windowsill to cool, Tink asked her if she had any pots, pans, spoons, whisks, or other kitchen items that she needed to get rid of.

"Well," replied Dulcie, "there was that salad fork with the bent tines. I was ready to give up on it. But Angus fixed it last week. It's been perfectly pointy and prongy ever since."

The other pots-and-pans fairies are too good at their jobs, Tink thought. She tugged at her fringe and gave a frustrated sigh. She didn't want to make a chair out of objects that were still useful.

Tink could usually fix almost anything. But here was something that couldn't be fixed, at least not right away.

"Grrr!" cried Tink. She shot three inches into the air with sheer frustration. Her room was smashed, and even when it was fixed, it still wouldn't feel like her room. After all, *where* was she going to find another loaf-pan bed?

That cannonball will regret the day it fell into Pixie Hollow, Tink vowed. *And Captain Hook will regret it even more.*

7

TINK ZOOMED into the courtyard. She flew right up to the cannonball and gave it a mighty kick.

Ow! Tink danced through the air, clutching her toes and grimacing in pain. A few fairies who had been flying by stared at Tink in astonishment.

Once her toes stopped hurting, Tink found that she felt much calmer. But now she was more determined than ever to get rid of the big, bad ball.

"This cannonball is going to move!" she cried. "I am going to banish it from Pixie Hollow once and for all. But I'm going to need help from every fairy and sparrow man. Together, we can do it! Now, who's with me?"

But the other fairies didn't jump up as Tink hoped they would.

"I don't know. Maybe we could learn to live with the cannonball," said one of the decoration-talent fairies. "We could probably fix it up to make it look nice."

The other decoration-talent fairies brightened a bit. "We could!" one agreed. "We could decorate it with hollyhock garlands and daisy chains."

"Or we could paint it a pretty shade of green to sort of blend in," said another. "Maybe a nice sage colour."

"But... but don't you want to get rid of it?" Tink asked, astonished.

"Well, of course we do, Tink," said Beck, who happened to be in the courtyard. "But we want to get back to doing what we usually do. We're all busy with our own talents."

Tink couldn't believe what she was hearing. Were the other fairies giving up already, before they'd even tried?

"We have fun in the courtyard, don't we?" she said. "It's part of our home. How will we feel looking at this cannonball every time we come out of the Home Tree? We'll never be able to have a meeting or a party here again. Even if it's decorated and painted, it will still take up too much room."

Several fairies murmured in agreement. But no one volunteered to help.

"We tried moving it yesterday, and we couldn't," a water-talent sparrow man pointed out.

"I know we can do this," Tink

replied. "We just have to figure out how."

Just then, Terence flew up. He was holding a teacup in one hand. In his other hand was a sack of fairy dust.

"Tink, you didn't get your fairy dust yet today, did you?" he said.

As a dust-talent sparrow man, Terence handed out dust to everyone in Pixie Hollow. They got one teacupful per day. The dust was what allowed the fairies to fly and do magic.

As Terence poured the magical dust over Tink, her eyes widened. "That's it! I know how we can move the cannonball!" she cried.

The fairies in the courtyard perked up. "How, Tink?" Terence asked.

"We move big things with balloon carriers, right?" Tink said. Balloon carriers were baskets attached to fairy-dust-filled balloons. The fairies used them to move things that were too heavy to carry. "That's what we'll do with the cannonball. We'll build a giant balloon and use lots of extra fairy dust to give it more lift. We can float the cannonball away."

"It's a good idea," said Terence. The other fairies nodded. Even Angus looked impressed.

"Send word to the other dust-talent fairies," Tink told Terence. "We'll need all the fairy dust they can spare. The rest of us will get the balloon carrier ready."

This was easier said than done. In order to attach the balloon to the cannonball, they would need heavy ropes. Tink found Florian and explained her plan.

"We'll use marsh grass this time," Florian said with certainty. "And we'll make it extra thick."

She got the weaving-talent fairies together, and they set out to collect long strands of tough marsh grasses, which they would weave into the strongest ropes they could make.

Next, Tink went to the sewing-talent fairies. She asked them to make a spider-silk balloon, the biggest one Pixie Hollow had ever seen.

It was afternoon by the time the weaving-talent fairies finished making the ropes. But they looked sturdy this time. They were nearly as thick as a fairy's waist.

The weavers secured the ropes

around the bottom of the cannonball. Then it was time to attach the balloon. The sewing-talent fairies sewed the ends of each rope to the edges of the balloon.

At last, the whole contraption was ready to go. It was time for the dust-talent fairies and sparrow men to do their work.

By now a crowd had gathered. Everyone watched, hardly daring to breathe, as Terence and a dust-talent sparrow man named Jerome began to fill the balloon with fairy dust. Instead of the teacups they usually used to hand out the dust, they scooped up great mounds of it with spades they had borrowed from the garden-talent fairies.

The balloon started to rise – up, up, up. The fairies watched in wonder. Soon the balloon was completely inflated. It strained against the ropes.

The ropes pulled taut, but the cannonball stayed stubbornly on the ground.

"More fairy dust!" cried Tink.

Terence and Jerome flew up to the top of the balloon and sprinkled more spadefuls of dust onto it. They sprinkled some dust onto the cannonball for good measure. The balloon strained harder and harder. All the fairies and sparrow men strained with it. Their muscles were tense. Their wings vibrated in sheer concentration. The fairies glowed brightly as they willed the balloon to rise.

And finally, it did! The grass ropes pulled tauter, and the cannonball could resist no longer. It lifted off the ground.

"It's going!" shouted Tink.

First it rose just a hair off the ground, no more than the thickness of a fairy's wing. Then it reached the height of two hairs. Then it was almost as high up as a fairy's knee, and then higher than a fairy's head. It was working! It was really working!

If the fairies and sparrow men had not been so caught up in the progress of the cannonball, they might have noticed that a strong breeze had sprung up. But they did not notice, until –

Pow!

Hisssssss.

"What was that?" Tink cried in alarm.

What it was, they soon discovered,

was a horse chestnut. The spiky green globe had fallen from a nearby horse chestnut tree. And the wind had been blowing in just the right direction to push it into the balloon. The horse chestnut's spikes had pierced the delicate spider silk.

The hissing lasted only a second. The cannonball landed back in the courtyard with a great thud. Inside the tree, delicate cups and saucers could be heard shattering in the tearoom.

The fairies groaned.

"Well, that's the end of that," Angus said.

But that wasn't the end. For the cannonball had got just the start it needed. It began to roll.

8

"THE BALL!" Rani cried. "L-look out!"

Several fairies leaped out of the way just in time. There was a very slight slope away from the Home Tree, but that was enough. The cannonball rolled down it.

"Hooray!" a decoration-talent fairy yelled. "Goodbye, ball!"

"Good riddance!" added a butterfly herder. Other fairies joined in the cheering.

But Tink followed the ball's progress, frowning.

"It's great that we got it going, but – " she began.

"Now we don't know *where* it's going," Rani finished for her.

"Exactly," said Tink.

The ball began to pick up speed. The fairies' cheers died out.

"It was so hard to start," Terence said worriedly. "But now it's going to be impossible to stop!"

"Maybe it will just roll into a tree or something," said Beck.

"If we're lucky," said Angus.

"I think we'd better follow it!" cried Tink. And the fairies leaped into the air to chase after the ball.

The cannonball was rolling fast now. It bounced across a tree root and rolled over a hillock of grass. It was headed for Havendish Stream.

"It's going to hit the mill!" cried Jerome.

This was truly a disaster. The mill was one of the most important places in

Pixie Hollow. The tree-picking-talent fairies ground grains and nuts into baking flour there. And the dust-talent fairies used the mill to grind Mother Dove's feathers into fairy dust. It was also where the fairy dust was stored – all of it. An entire year's supply.

At once, the same picture flashed through every fairy and sparrow man's mind: the mill smashed, the fairy dust inside blowing away with the wind. They would be unable to fly, unable to do magic. How would they even build another mill if they did not have the power of fairy dust?

A startled rabbit poked his head out of his burrow. But when he saw the cannonball rolling towards him, he quickly dove back inside.

The cannonball rolled over a large toadstool, flattening it. The fairies flew helplessly behind. They could hardly bring themselves to watch.

But just before it reached the mill, the cannonball hit a good-sized rock. It jumped into the air and changed course. Instead of crashing into the mill, the ball splashed into the stream just above it. And there it stopped, wedged against the bank.

The fairies breathed sighs of relief all around. They laughed and hugged each other with joy. The mill was saved!

But Tink was not laughing. She did not take her eyes from the ball. As she watched, the water of Havendish Stream began to back up around it.

"Oh, no!" she said. "The stream is

blocked!"

Everyone stared in disbelief. Tink was right. The ball had landed in the narrow branch of the stream that fed the mill. The water slowed to a trickle.

This was not good. Not good at all. If the stream stopped running, the mill wheel would stop turning.

Indeed, they all heard the mill grind to a stop.

Rani started to cry, and it was not from happiness.

Why didn't I think of this? Tink asked herself angrily. *Why didn't it occur to me that once the ball started rolling, it was anybody's guess where it would end up?*

She sank down to the ground. She felt completely defeated. She had taken on a challenge that was too big. And she had failed. What was going to happen to Pixie Hollow now?

"Well, Tink," someone said. Tink looked up. Queen Clarion was standing next to her. "I guess it's time for you to come up with another idea," the queen said seriously.

This took Tink by surprise. She had thought the story was over. The ball was stuck in the stream. There was certainly no way to move it now.

But Rani was nodding and smiling through her tears. "We know you can figure this out, Tink," she said. "Look how many things you've already thought of. There has to be one more thing."

Tink was astounded. Not only did the others have hope that the problem could be solved, they thought she could solve it.

Rani is right, she thought. *There has to be one more thing.* Tink knew she had a responsibility to work out what that one thing was. The other fairies were counting on her.

"Yes, Tink," said Florian. "It's time for your next idea. Do you want us to leave you alone?"

"Or would you like some nice soup while you think?" said one of the cooking-talent fairies, who specialised in cucumber soup.

"No soup," Tink said, squaring her shoulders. "I'm just going to think."

9

TINK FLITTED around the whole terrible scene, trying to focus. It was hard looking at the mess the cannonball had made. Water was starting to flood the banks of the stream, turning them into muddy pools. Toadstools and wildflowers had been squashed and flattened when the ball rolled over them. The cannonball had also plowed through a pile of acorns that the tree-picking-talent fairies had set aside to be ground in the mill. Now little chips of acorn littered the landscape.

Tink stared at them. They reminded her of something.

Little chips of acorn, she thought. *Little chips…*

"I've got it!" she hollered. "I've got

the solution! I was thinking about it the wrong way the whole time! The cannonball is a huge thing, right?" said Tink. "It was much too heavy for us to move. And we certainly couldn't control it once it started moving. But even if we can't move a huge thing, we can move lots of *little* things."

Queen Ree nodded her head in understanding. "Of course!" she said.

"Of course *what?*" said a few fairies who hadn't caught on.

"We're going to break the cannonball into lots of tiny pieces and move them out of Pixie Hollow," Tink declared.

"Spring!" She turned to the message-talent fairy. "Ask the other pots-and-pans fairies to bring all the hammers and chisels they have in their workshops. And the carpenter-talent fairies – they have hammers and chisels, too!"

"I have a couple of chisels," said an art-talent fairy. "For making sculptures."

"Great!" said Tink. "Let's round up all the tools we have. We're going to break this cannonball up!"

A short time later, an array of tools was laid out on the grass next to the cannonball. The sand-sorting-talent fairies had piled sandbags around the ball, to hold back the stream. That way, the fairies wouldn't get wet as they worked.

Tink grabbed a hammer and chisel and flew to the top of the cannonball. As the best pots-and-pans fairy in Pixie Hollow, Tink knew a lot about metal. For example, she knew that every piece of metal had a weak point.

She put her ear close to the cannonball. Then she began to tap it with her hammer, inching across the surface.

Bing, bing, bing, bing, bong, bing…

Tink stopped. She went back and tapped the spot again.

Bong!

Tink had found the cannonball's weak spot. Holding the tip of her chisel against the ball, Tink whacked it with the hammer as hard as she could. A crack appeared.

Tink whacked it again. The crack grew.

"Everybody take a hammer and chisel!" Tink told the other fairies. "Even if your talent is completely unrelated to breaking up cannonballs, give it a try. You might like it."

The fairies got to work. As they wedged their chisels into the iron, more cracks appeared. The air started to ring with the sound of metal banging into metal. It was a sound Tink loved with all her heart.

"I like this!" said one of the cooking-talent fairies, whose specialty was making ice sculptures. "It's just like chipping ice. But you don't have to be careful!"

Gradually, the cracks in the cannonball grew. Pieces began to break off. The fairies laid them on the bank of Havendish Stream.

Soon they had broken the whole cannonball apart. A mound of iron bits sat by the stream.

"What are we going to do with all this?" said Twire, a scrap-metal-recovery-talent fairy. "It's more iron than we could use in an entire year in Pixie Hollow."

Tink nodded. But she wasn't really focused on what Twire was saying. She was getting another idea.

Quietly, she waved Terence over. "I want to ask your opinion about something," she said. "About fairy-dust magic." She whispered her idea into Terence's ear.

Terence scratched his head thoughtfully.

"I think it can be done," he said finally. "It will take a great deal of fairy dust. And the magic won't be easy. We'll have to concentrate. But I think it could work."

"That's what I hoped," said Tink.

She flew back to where the other fairies were still working. They were almost finished breaking apart the cannonball.

Tink stood on one of the bigger pieces of iron to make her announcement.

"Fairies," she said, "we're going to get this cannonball out of Pixie Hollow once and for all."

The fairies cheered.

"But what are we going to do with it?" asked Rani.

Tink smiled and said with a wink, "We're going to give it back to Captain Hook, of course."

10

SHOUTING WITH GLEE, the fairies gathered up the pieces of cannonball. There were many more pieces than there were fairies. So each fairy took as many as she could fly with. Gwinn took one big piece. Cedar took six small ones. Tink herself carried three pieces, and it took all her strength to lift off.

Meanwhile, Jerome and Terence were inside the mill filling sacks full of fairy dust, as much as they could carry.

When everything was ready, the fairies lifted into the air. It was quite a sight, for those who could see it: a great cloud of fairies flying over the lush landscape of Never Land, headed for Pirate Cove. Of course, the pirates themselves could not see the fairies, who were invisible to them. If Captain Hook had looked up just then, he would have seen hundreds of chips of iron miraculously bobbing through the air.

But Captain Hook was not looking up. As the fairies approached the cove, they could see the vile-tempered pirate rowing a small boat through the water near the shore. He was muttering to himself.

"I'll teach that ridiculous boy a lesson," he growled. "Throw my best cutlass into the sea, will he? Thinks he can get the best of me, does he? Well, we'll see about that, Master Peter Pan. Let's see how you like a cannonball for your dinner tonight."

As Hook rowed, he looked down through the shallow water. Evidently, he was trying to find his lost cutlass.

The fairies were right above Hook's little boat. They hovered there, still in a cloud. "Okay!" Tink cried. "Start bringing the pieces together!"

The fairies flew nearer to each other. They began to fit the pieces of cannonball together.

"Now the fairy dust!" Tink commanded.

Terence and the other dust-talent fairies and sparrow men began to throw handfuls of fairy dust over the ball. Magically, the iron chips snapped into place like pieces of a jigsaw puzzle. The fairies concentrated, using all the magic they could muster.

In moments, the cannonball was complete. It was just as it had been when it crashed into Pixie Hollow.

And, of course, once it was whole, it was too heavy for the fairies to hold any longer. It fell from their grasp and plummeted towards Captain Hook's rowing boat.

Hook looked up just in time to see a cannonball fall from thin air.

"What – " was all he had time to say before the ball crashed into the floor of his boat. It broke through the wood and fell to the bottom of the sea.

At once, the boat filled with water. Hook had no choice but to abandon ship. He swam to shore as the boat slowly sank.

The sun was setting as the fairies flew back to Pixie Hollow, glad to finally be rid of the cannonball.

The next day, Pixie Hollow had just about returned to normal. Havendish Stream flowed between its banks, which looked none the worse for wear. The mill was turning once again. And fairies from several different talents had pitched in to help repair the courtyard.

The cooking-talent fairies had spent the day making acorn soup, muffins, cookies, and bread with the acorns that had been smashed by the cannonball. Everyone was sick of acorns. But all the broken ones had been just about used up, and nothing had gone to waste.

After her wet night in Rani's room, Tink had decided to sleep outside until her room was rebuilt. She'd found a nook between two branches where she would be sheltered from the wind and safe from owls. She had actually been quite happy out there, looking at the stars through the leaves of the Home Tree.

And in the morning, what had she found by the roots of a nearby tree but her loaf-pan bed! It had one big dent in it. *Challenging to fix*, Tink thought. *But not too challenging.*

Later that day, Gwinn and Cedar helped Tink carry the bed up to her new room. They had worked all night to get it ready for her.

When Gwinn opened the door, Tink was speechless with delight. Her new room had colander lamps just like the old ones. The walls were painted with silver paint to make them look as if they were made of tin. And best of all, Bess had manged to finish a new painting for Tink after all. It was another still life of a stockpot, whisk, and griddle – and it was twice the size of the old one.

"It's beautiful," she managed to say at last.

Gwinn and Cedar helped Tink put her bed back into place. Then Gwinn took another look around the room. "You know," she said thoughtfully, "we could decorate with tiny cannonballs, Tink. So you'd always remember your greatest challenge."

"It's an interesting thought," said Tink. "But I'm all through with cannonballs."

Just then, Dulcie came hurrying up to Tink's room. She poked her head in the open door and waved a metal sheet.

"Tink," she said, "do you think you could fix this baking sheet for me? I have one last batch of acorn cookies to put in the oven. It just has a little hole. I know it's hardly worth your attention. Not much of a challenge."

"Believe me," said Tink, "that is just fine with me."

And taking the sheet from Dulcie's hands, she headed for her workshop, whistling.